Sophie
and Sammy's
Library
Sleepover

JUDITH CASELEY

Sophie and Sammy's

Library Sleepover

Greenwillow Books, New York

Watercolor paints and colored pencils
were used for the full-color art.
The text type is Bryn Mawr Book.

Printed in Singapore by Tien Wah Press
First Edition
10 9 8 7 6 5 4 3 2 1

Library of Congress Cataloging-in-Publication Data

Caseley, Judith.
Sophie and Sammy's library sleepover / by Judith Caseley.
p.   cm.
Summary: A loving and sensitive book-loving
little girl teaches her brother to enjoy books.
ISBN 0-688-10615-3
ISBN 0-688-10616-1 [lib.]
[1. Books and reading—Fiction.
2. Brothers and sisters—Fiction.]
I. Title.
PZ7.C2677So   1993
[E]—dc20
91-48160   CIP   AC

Queens Library
Hillcrest Branch
187-05 Union Turnpike
Flushing, New York
JUL 9
JUL 31
SEP 10
OCT 31
DEC 11
OCT 18
JAN 14
JAN 19
FEB 2
FEB 23
To children's librarians everywhere...
SORRY NO RENEWALS

Sophie and Sammy loved books.
Sophie loved to read them.
Sammy loved to rip them and
write on them
and throw them
and step on them.

So Sammy's mother took them away
from him.
"When you learn how to treat books
the way your sister does,"
said his mother, "you can have
them back."
"How does Sophie treat them?"
said Sammy.
"Like friends," said
his mother.

So Sophie and Sammy painted pictures or played
with their toys or watched cartoons on television.
Whenever Sophie got bored, she read her books.
(Sammy just stayed bored.)

"This book is about an elephant like Igor," she told Sammy.
"I know how much you love elephants."
"So what," said Sammy, even though elephants
and scary monsters were just about his
favorite things in the whole world.

One evening Sammy's mother gave them both a bath.
After they brushed their teeth, she told Sophie to put
on her best pajamas and pick out her favorite stuffed
animal.

"I'm taking Sophie on a surprise visit," said her mother.

"What about me?" said Sammy.

"When you're older," said his mother.

Sophie and her pet tiger, Stripes, went in
the car with her mother, and Sammy stayed
home with his father.
They drove for a while and parked in front
of a large brick building. It was dark
outside, so it was hard to see.
"It's the library!" said Sophie when they
walked inside.

They found the reading room.
There were lots of other children
there, dressed in all sorts of
pajamas and nightgowns and
carrying all kinds of dolls and animals.
"Sammy would have brought Igor," Sophie
whispered to her mother.

They sat in a circle and waited. Finally, in walked the librarian, Mrs. Terry, wearing a long nightgown and bunny slippers and holding a toy monkey. She sat down on the floor and said, "Good evening, boys and girls. Welcome to my library sleepover. You won't really be spending the night here, but by reading books and using our imaginations, we can pretend all sorts of things."

Then Mrs. Terry lit
a candle and said,
"When this candle burns out,
storytime is over."

The first book Mrs. Terry read was about a chimpanzee
who lived in the jungle.
"Sammy would have liked this story," Sophie whispered
to her mother. "Igor is a jungle elephant."

Sophie and the children made believe they were
swinging from branches until the librarian said,
"Shhhh. It's time for bed now."

Her bedtime book was about a little girl who
was afraid to go to sleep because she thought
there was a monster on the roof.
"I hear footsteps," whispered Mrs. Terry. "Let's
cover our eyes."

Sophie covered her eyes. Mrs. Terry made the story
sound so scary that Sophie thought she heard funny
noises coming from the ceiling.

She peeked to see if her mother was frightened.
Her mother was peeking at Sophie,
and they started to laugh.
"Sammy loves getting scared," whispered Sophie
in between giggles.

Mrs. Terry finished the story and said, "Let's get
into our beds." She pretended she was covering
herself with blankets. Mrs. Terry looked very cozy,
even though they weren't real blankets.
Sophie and the children made themselves cozy, too.
Then Mrs. Terry read them a story about a little boy
who couldn't fall asleep without his favorite blanket.

Mrs. Terry finished the story. "I'm so very sleepy," she said, rubbing her eyes and yawning until the children felt like yawning, too. She sang "Rockabye Baby," and at the end the children all fell down, even though Mrs. Terry didn't tell them to.

"Sammy would have liked this part the best," said Sophie to her mother.

At last the candle burned out. The children
gathered up their stuffed animals, and Mrs. Terry
whispered, "That's the end of our sleepover.
Good night, sleep tight."
"Good night, sleep tight," the children whispered back.

Sophie was quiet on the way home in the car.
She nodded her head when her mother asked her
if she had enjoyed the library sleepover. She didn't
make a peep when her mother tucked her into
bed without reading her a single book.

Sophie's mother kissed her good night. "Didn't we
have fun at the library sleepover?" she said.

"It was great," said Sophie, but she had a funny
look on her face.

"What's the matter, honey?" said her mother.

"We should have brought Sammy," said Sophie.
It was Sophie's mother's turn to be quiet.
Finally she said, "I think you're right. But it's
too late now."

Sophie didn't think so. She had an idea, and
she told her mother about it.

The very next evening, Sophie and Sammy had
their baths and got into their pajamas.
"Come with me," said Sophie, "and bring Igor."
She led Sammy into her bedroom. On the floor
was a mattress surrounded by books.
"It's a book bed," said Sophie, and they climbed
into bed. "This is our library sleepover," she said.
"Only it's in our own house."

Sophie took out a flashlight. "Mommy wouldn't let me use a candle," she said. Then Sophie read Sammy every book that she knew how to read. At last Sophie told the story about the monster on the roof. She made it so scary that Sammy pulled the covers over his head.

"I hear footsteps," whispered Sophie, just the way
 Mrs. Terry had.
"In the hallway," whispered Sammy, peeking out.
 The bedroom door opened slowly.
 Sophie saw a furry foot.
 Sammy saw a hand, holding something.

"It looks like a claw!" whispered Sammy.
"Holding a poison drink!" whispered Sophie.
"It's the monster!" screamed Sammy.

"It's Mommy," said Sophie, "with milk and cookies!"
"I thought all that reading might have made you
  hungry," said their mother.
Sammy agreed. Then he munched on a cookie and
said to his mother, "I'm ready to have my books
back now."

The next night, and every night after that,
Sophie and Sammy had a library sleepover...
in Sophie's bed, with the lights on, without
a flashlight. Sophie said she wanted to be
a librarian when she grew up.